GERIBO,

The Shelter Cat

CLAIRE ECKARD

Illustrated by Erin Amavisca

Mill City Press

Mill City Press, Inc.
2301 Lucien Way #415
Maitland, FL 32751
407.339.4217
www.millcitypress.net

Illustrated by Erin Amavisca

Printed in the United States of America

Paperback ISBN-13: 978-1-6628-1025-1
Hard Cover ISBN-13: 978-1-6628-1026-8
Ebook ISBN-13: 978-1-6628-1027-5

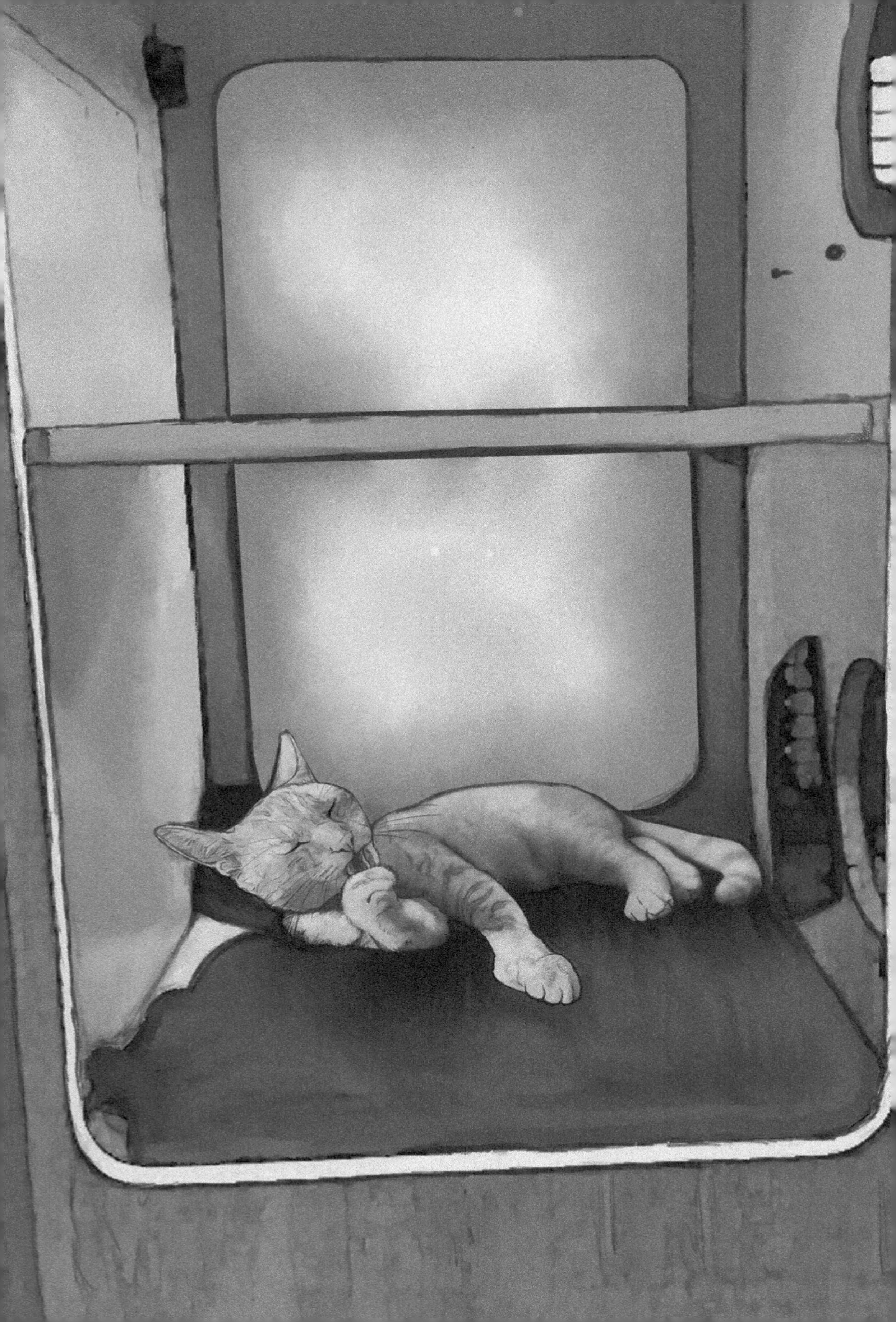

Geribo had been at the shelter for a hundred days.

Today, the shelter staff were planning on doing a special photograph of Geribo to put on Facebook and on their website to help him get adopted!

Geribo was really hoping someone would see his picture and want to give him a forever home!

He had spent all morning grooming himself with his rough tongue so that he looked his very best!

The people at the shelter were very kind to Geribo, but he did not like sitting in the cage all by himself. He would rather be getting cuddled by his very own person. He would also like to have a fluffy cat bed of his own.

Each cat had its' own cat condo with room to sleep, eat, and go to the bathroom. It was not very private though!

At 10am Loma, one of the shelter's wonderful volunteers, came to get Geribo from his cage. Loma told him what a nice boy he was, and that she could not imagine why he hadn't been adopted yet.

When Loma said that, Geribo felt very sad. He thought he knew why he had not been adopted. It was because of his very large front paws! When Geribo was a little kitten he could remember his siblings laughing at him.

Geribo wondered if he hadn't been adopted because he looked different from the other cats.

Loma carried Geribo to the room where they took the photographs of all the animals available for adoption. There were lots of fun props and costumes to dress the animals up in.

All the people who helped with the photographs were volunteers. A volunteer is a person who helps others without getting paid for what they do. They help because they want to do something nice for the animals.

Today Loma was the photographer, and Erin and Popi-Mary were the animal "wranglers." The animal wrangler would get the dog or cat ready for the photograph. Geribo was determined to be a very well-behaved cat today, and not fidget and fuss!

Loma and Popi-Mary decided that Geribo would look very handsome as a cowboy! When it was his turn to have his picture taken, he stood up very tall and straight, and even tried to smile for the camera! How do you think his picture turned out?

Once they were done, Geribo decided to sneak off and explore the shelter!

First, he wandered into Annette's office. Annette was the Director of the shelter. Geribo jumped right up onto her desk!

Annette laughed and showed Geribo what she was doing on her computer. It was a project that would teach children at a local school how important it is to take care of their pets. She also wanted them to understand that if the pet had a microchip it would be much easier to find if it was lost.

A microchip is a teeny, tiny, thing about the size of a grain of rice. It is placed under the skin of the animal by a vet.

The microchip can then be scanned if the pet is lost and ends up at an animal shelter. The shelter staff can read the information on the microchip which will tell them the pet's name, who the pet belongs to, and gives the contact information of the owner.

Geribo then went to visit Trentie in the foster department. Trentie had a team of foster parents who would take animals into their homes that were too young or too sick to be in the shelter.

Trentie always had cute little puppies and kittens in her office. Geribo jumped into the playpen with them and was soon having a fun game of Roly-Poly, being extra careful that his big paws would not hurt any of the babies. Then they all took a little nap together!

DOG FOOD
IT TAKES A COMMUNITY!

After his nap Geribo kept looking around until he found Lana's office. Lana was in charge of fundraising, which meant that she had to make sure there was enough money to feed and care for all the animals at the Shelter.

Sometimes Lana would ask people to donate items the animals needed. Can you see In the picture what some of those items might be?

TICKETS AVAILABLE AT:
OUR SHELTER & THRIFT STORE

www.helpthepets.com

ALL PROCEEDS BENEFIT
THE SHELTER PETS

Lana also helped to plan events to raise money for the shelter. People could buy a ticket to an event and enjoy a lovely night of dinner and dancing, for example.

Geribo was very impressed at all the hard-working staff at the shelter. He had not realized how many people it took to care for the animals and find them new homes.

Next, Geribo strolled over to the adoption room where a counselor would meet with a family that had seen an animal they would like to take home with them.

The adoption counselor would make sure they were prepared to give their new pet a forever home, because animals do not like to leave their homes and their families. They want to stay with them their whole lives.

Alyssa, the adoptions counselor, was sitting with an elderly man who was looking for a senior dog to adopt.

A senior dog is older and might be a little slow and stiff, but senior dogs and cats still have lots of love to give.

The elderly man told Alyssa that he could not take a dog for long walks anymore, but he would make sure the dog was loved, had plenty of cuddles, and lots of good food and company. He had seen a dog called Samson on the shelter website and thought he might be perfect.

Geribo jumped up onto Alyssa's desk to watch what happened, while one of the staff members went to get Samson out of his kennel.

When Samson arrived at Alyssa's office, he looked a little confused. Geribo watched as the elderly man smiled at Samson and reached out his hand. Samson sniffed his fingers and allowed the man to pet him. Soon he was resting his head on the old man's lap and getting scratched behind his ears.

Before long, Samson was wagging his tail and hoping he would be able to stay a little longer with this nice person.

Geribo could tell they all liked each other a lot and he was sure that Samson had found his forever home, but Samson had not realized that yet!

Once the adoption paperwork was done, the elderly man stood up and spoke to Samson,

“Are you ready to go home now, fella?” he asked.

Samson was still confused. Was the man going to put him back in his kennel now?

Alyssa gave Samson a big hug.

"Congratulations, Samson; you have found your forever home and someone who will love you forever."

Suddenly Samson realized what was happening. His sad old eyes became bright, and his tired old body hopped around in excitement. He was going home!!!!!

Samson was so happy. He had almost given up on finding another family of his own. Some of the shelter staff cried tears of happiness as they watched Samson walk out of the shelter forever.

This was why the staff and volunteers work so hard, Geribo thought. They just want to see every animal find a loving home. Geribo looked down at his big paws and wondered if he would ever find his forever family.

Geribo knew he had lots of love to give. If he could ever find a family of his own he would try really hard not to let his big paws get in the way or be a nuisance.

I won a
trip on the
Resc
Exp

Just then Loma appeared in Alyssa's doorway.

"I have a surprise for you, Geribo!" she said.

Loma carried Geribo over to Miss Cathy's office. Miss Cathy's job was to send some of the shelter animals to rescue organizations in other cities. Going to a rescue was one step closer to a pet finding his or her forever home!

Guess who had been chosen to go today? You guessed it! Geribo!!!!!

Miss Cathy gave Geribo a sticker that said, "I won a ticket on the Rescue Express." He purred extra loudly and everyone laughed!

Since it would be his last night at the shelter Annette told Loma that Geribo could stay in her office for the night instead of going back to his cage.

When Annette left to go home Geribo was all snuggled up in a cozy cat bed with a nice bowl of food and water next to him.

“Goodnight Geribo,” she said, as she turned off the light to her office.

“Sweet dreams!”

Geribo closed his eyes and did indeed have very sweet dreams. In his dream he was being cuddled by a lovely little girl who was giving him kisses and telling him how very much she loved him.

Geribo's big paws were right there where she could see them, and she loved him anyway! Maybe there really was a forever home out there for Geribo!

While Samson slept soundly in his new home, Geribo purred happily in his sleep, knowing that tomorrow his own new adventures will begin!

Claire Eckard
Author

Claire Eckard has been an animal lover her whole life, which is reflected in many of her children's books. She was on the Board of The Humane Society of Yuma for 6 years and is passionate about educating children regarding the care and responsibility of animals in their community. Claire lives on a ranch near Prescott, Arizona with her husband, 10 horses, 3 dogs and a miniature mule!

Erin Amavisca
Illustrator

Erin worked as a marketing manager for a local shelter and now is a full-time art teacher in West Virginia. She was born with a love of animals and with art in her soul. Erin finds endless inspiration in her daughter Kayden! Erin lives on her ranch in Bunker Hill with her husband, daughter, 3 horses, 4 cats, 2 dogs, 5 chickens and 2 fish! The images of Geribo are based on her cat Willy Nelson!

Hello! This is Claire Eckard. I wrote the book you just read about Geribo, the Shelter Cat. I have some questions for you! There are no right or wrong answers, these are just some things to think about!

1. Do you have an animal shelter or rescue in your community? Often they have events that children can go to which help to raise money for the shelter animals. Maybe you could go to one!

2. Why do you think Geribo was so sure his big paws were stopping him from being adopted? All animals, and all people are unique. Sometimes it is what is different about us that makes us so special!

3. Geribo often thinks about having a special person of his own to love him. Do you have a pet? Do you know how important it is for that pet to feel safe and loved? What do you love most about your pet?

4. Samson is a senior dog and he is so sad to have lost his family. Maybe his owner died or got sick and could no longer care for him. Were you happy when he realized he had found a new home? What do you think he looked forward to the most about having a home and family again?

5. There are so many animals waiting for homes in animal shelters across the country. When you grow up, or when your family is looking for a new pet, do you think you can give a home to one of these animals?

I think we are all excited to see if Geribo finds his special person and his forever home! Look for the next book in the Geribo series – Geribo and the Rescue Express, coming Christmas 2021!!

CPSIA information can be obtained
at www.ICGtesting.com
Printed in the USA
LVHW070841060621
689465LV00013B/506

9 781662 81025